To Jessica
with love from.

Harriet

For Ferd Monjo R.H.

For Daniel M.B.

First published 1984 by Walker Books Ltd,
17-19 Hanway House,
Hanway Place, London W1P 9DL

First printed 1984
Printed and bound by L.E.G.O., Vicenza, Italy

British Library Cataloguing in Publication Data
Hoban, Russell
Lavinia Bat. – (Ponders; v.4)
I. Title II. Baynton, Martin III. Series
823'.914[J] PZ7

ISBN 0-7445-0077-X

LAVINIA BAT

RUSSELL HOBAN

Illustrated by
MARTIN BAYNTON

WALKER BOOKS
LONDON

Hanging head down in her winter sleep Lavinia Bat was quite comfortable. Her winter dreams were always pleasant, always slow, never hurried.

In her dream the night was a lantern-globe of sound, it was lit with the colour of the wind, the rolling of the earth, the starfires of crickets. It made a gentle hissing as it turned in space and all its skies turned with it.

Lavinia woke up, still half in her dream. She washed herself and stretched her wings and did her waking-up exercises. She flew up and down her cave, she did loops and turns, she did rolls and dives and figure eights. Then she went back to sleep.

In her dream Lavinia heard a whispering, she listened to it carefully.

'Pass it on,' said the whispering.

'Pass what on?' said Lavinia.

'The something from the other,' said the whispering.

'What other?' said Lavinia.

'The other dream,' said the whispering.

Nights and days passed, the moon grew fat, grew thin, grew fat, grew thin. The skunk cabbages pushed up green points out of the ground, then the Jack-in-the-pulpits stood up in the boggy places and Big John Turkle climbed onto a log and tried out the sunlight.

Lavinia woke up. All she could remember was 'Pass it on'. But she couldn't remember what the something was that she was meant to pass on.

It was evening, it was spring, it was time to get moving. Outside the cave everything smelled wet and muddy and new.

What a singing there was at the pond! Jugs-of-rum were sung by the bullfrogs while others claimed that the water was only knee-deep, knee-deep. The peepers peeped constantly but they never told what they saw. 'We peep, we peep!' was all they would say. Some of the insects said that Katy did, some said that Katy didn't, no one knew for sure.

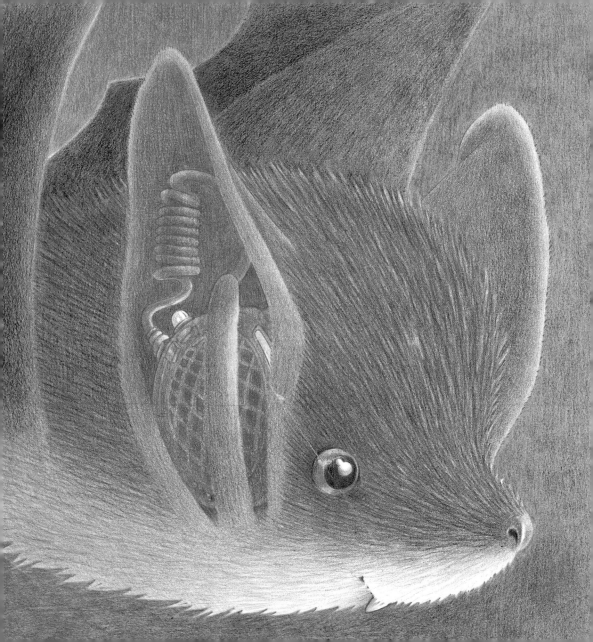

Lavinia put her FM echolocator on SCAN, she put her computer on AUTOMATIC and she was ready to go. Other bats were coming out as well, all frequency bands were clicking and buzzing as they scrambled skitter-scattering, cornering into the night, they hadn't eaten since autumn.

What a skirmish for supper! The darkness was full of buzzing, whirring, and flapping things to eat.

'CLICK CLICK CLICK CLICK CLICK,' went
Lavinia's scanner as it made its sweep,
'BZZZZZZZZZ!' as she zeroed in on her
prey. Fat moths looped and turned and
rolled and dived and Lavinia looped and
turned and rolled and dived with them,
some she caught and some she missed.

'JUG-OF-RUM!' sang Jim Frog and
his crowd.
'Knee-deep!' sang the others.
'We peep!' sang the peepers.
'Katy did!' sang the katydids.
'Katy didn't!' sang the katydidn'ts.
'WHOOHOOHOO!' hooted Ephraim Owl.
'BLEAK OUTLO news and weather!'
whispered Charlie Meadows.

'MOTH AT SIX O'CLOCK!' said Lavinia's scanner. 'FOUR METRES AND CLOSING, THREE METRES, TWO...'

'DIVE!' said Lavinia's computer.

'I TASTE AWFUL!' ultrasounded the moth.

'Ptui!' said Lavinia, zooming up out of her dive and zeroing in on another moth.

'I TASTE AWFUL TOO!' ultrasounded that one.

'No, you don't,' said Lavinia. SCHLOOP!

What a supper that was, the first night of the spring outcoming!

Lavinia was listening to the night all round her and she was listening inside herself as well. She was going to have a baby.

'Ah!' said Lavinia, clicking to herself. She half-remembered something but she half-forgot it at the same time.

When Lavinia's time came her baby was born, it was a daughter and Lavinia named her Lola.

Lola was clever, she wanted to know about everything. She said to Lavinia, 'How do you do bat work?'

Lavinia said, 'Hang on and I'll show you.'

Lola hung on and Lavinia showed her.

'The main thing,' said Lavinia, 'is to get tuned in.'

'Tuned in to what?' said Lola.

'Everything,' said Lavinia. She took Lola hunting with her and Lola got tuned in. She got tuned in to the night, she got tuned in to moving with it. Soon Lola was ready to hunt for herself. Off she went, cornering into the night.

Lavinia remembered her dreams then, remembered the lantern-globe of night, the hissing of it as it turned in space. Lavinia remembered the whispering that had said, 'Pass it on!'

'Ah!' said Lavinia, clicking and buzzing, sweeping the night with her scanner and rolling with the rolling world.

'Ah!' said Lavinia, tuned into everything. 'I've done that!'